Cat Hen Duck Goose Dog  Sheep

 Pig Goat Cow Cat Hen Duck

Goose Dog Sheep  Pig Goat Cow

Cat Hen  Duck Goose Dog Sheep

Pig Goat Cow Cat Hen  Duck

Cat Hen Duck Goose Dog  Sheep

Pig Goat Cow Cat Hen Duck

Goose Dog Sheep Pig Goat Cow

Cat Hen Duck Goose Dog Sheep

Pig Goat Cow Cat Hen Duck

Fiddle-I-Fee

Fiddle-I-Fee

A Farmyard Song for the Very Young

Adapted and illustrated by Melissa Sweet

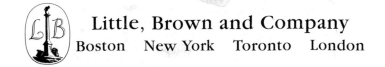

Little, Brown and Company
Boston   New York   Toronto   London

First Paperback Edition

Library of Congress Cataloging-in-Publication Data

Sweet, Melissa.
    Fiddle-I-fee : a farmyard song for the very young / [Melissa
Sweet]. — 1st ed.
        p.   cm.
    Summary: In this cumulative nursery rhyme and folk song,
a parade forms when several farm animals join a boy on his
journey around the farmyard.
    ISBN 0-316-82516-6 (hc)
    ISBN 0-316-82522-0 (pb)
    1. Folk-songs, American — Texts.   2. Children's songs,
American — Texts.   3. Nursery rhymes, American.
4. Children's poetry, American.   [1. Domestic animals —
Songs and music.   2. Folk songs, American.   3. Nursery
rhymes.]   I. Title.
PZ8.3.S99518Fi   1992
782.42162'13'00833 — dc20   90-40884

10   9   8   7   6   5   4   3

WOR

Published simultaneously in Canada
by Little, Brown & Company (Canada) Limited

Printed in the United States of America

to
Abbe

I had a cat
and the cat pleased me,
I fed my cat under yonder tree;

Cat went fiddle-i-fee.

I had a . . .

hen

and the hen pleased me,
I fed my hen under yonder tree;
Hen went chipsy-chopsy,

Cat went fiddle-i-fee.

I had a . . .

duck

and the duck pleased me,
I fed my duck under yonder tree;
Duck went quack, quack,

Hen went chipsy-chopsy,
Cat went fiddle-i-fee.

I had a . . .

goose

and the goose pleased me,
I fed my goose under yonder tree;
Goose went swishy-swashy,

Duck went quack, quack,
Hen went chipsy-chopsy,
Cat went fiddle-i-fee.

I had a . . .

dog

and the dog pleased me,
I fed my dog under yonder tree;
Dog went bow-wow, bow-wow,

Goose went swishy-swashy,
Duck went quack, quack,
Hen went chipsy-chopsy,
Cat went fiddle-i-fee.

I had a . . .

sheep

and the sheep pleased me,
I fed my sheep under yonder tree;
Sheep went baa, baa,

Dog went bow-wow, bow-wow,
Goose went swishy-swashy,
Duck went quack, quack,
Hen went chipsy-chopsy,
Cat went fiddle-i-fee.

I had a . . .

pig
and the pig pleased me,
I fed my pig under yonder tree;
Pig went griffy-gruffy,

Sheep went baa, baa,
Dog went bow-wow, bow-wow,
Goose went swishy-swashy,
Duck went quack, quack,
Hen went chipsy-chopsy,
Cat went fiddle-i-fee.

I had a . . .

goat

and the goat pleased me,
I fed my goat under yonder tree;
Goat went bleat, bleat,

Pig went griffy-gruffy,
Sheep went baa, baa,
Dog went bow-wow, bow-wow,
Goose went swishy-swashy,
Duck went quack, quack,
Hen went chipsy-chopsy,
Cat went fiddle-i-fee.

I had a . . .

COW

and the cow pleased me,
I fed my cow under yonder tree;
Cow went moo, moo . . .

Goat went bleat, bleat,
Pig went griffy-gruffy,
sheep went baa, baa,
Dog went bow-wow, bow-wow,
Goose went swishy-swashy,

Duck went quack, quack,
Hen went chipsy-chopsy,
Cat went . . .

fiddle

Fiddle-I-Fee

Traditional
Arranged by Alain Mallet

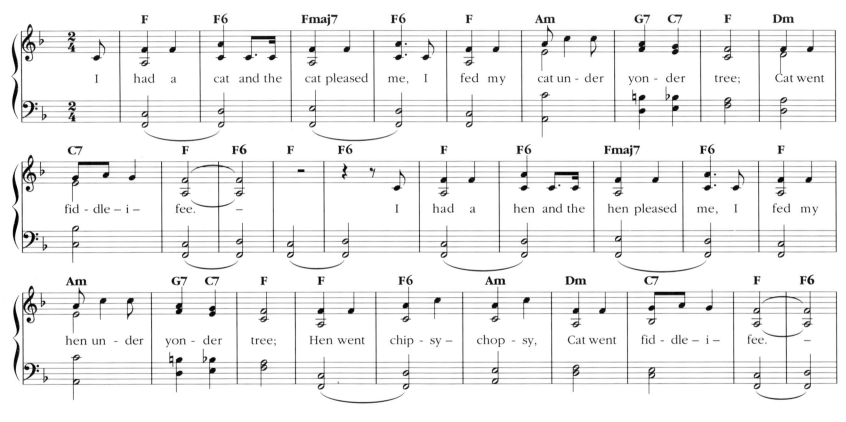

Lyrics:

I had a cat and the cat pleased me, I fed my cat un-der yon-der tree; Cat went fid-dle-i-fee. —

I had a hen and the hen pleased me, I fed my hen un-der yon-der tree; Hen went chip-sy-chop-sy, Cat went fid-dle-i-fee. —

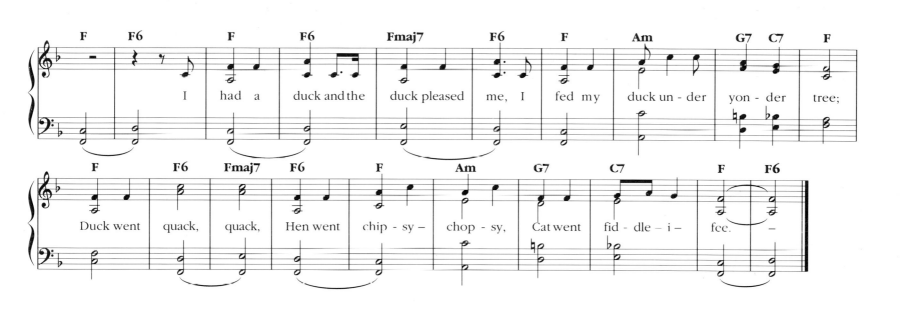

I had a duck and the duck pleased me, I fed my duck un - der yon - der tree;

Duck went quack, quack, Hen went chip - sy - chop - sy, Cat went fid - dle - i - fee. —

Cat Hen Duck Goose Dog  Sheep

Pig Goat Cow Cat Hen Duck

Goose Dog Sheep Pig Goat Cow

Cat Hen Duck Goose Dog Sheep

Pig Goat Cow Cat Hen Duck

at Hen Duck Goose Dog  Sheep

 Pig Goat Cow Cat Hen Duck

Goose Dog Sheep  Pig Goat Cow

Cat Hen  Duck Goose Dog Sheep

Pig Goat Cow Cat Hen  Duck